This book is a work of fiction. Any references to historical events, real people, or real places are used fictitiously. Other names, characters, places, and events are products of the author's imagination, and any resemblance to actual events or places or persons, living or dead, is entirely coincidental.

LITTLE SIMON
An imprint of Simon & Schuster Children's Publishing Division • 1230 Avenue of the Americas, New York, New York 10020 • First Little Simon hardcover edition June 2018 • Copyright © 2018 by Simon & Schuster, Inc. All rights reserved, including the right of reproduction in whole or in part in any form. LITTLE SIMON is a registered trademark of Simon & Schuster, Inc., and associated colophon is a trademark of Simon & Schuster, Inc. For information about special discounts for bulk purchases, please contact Simon & Schuster Special Sales at 1-866-506-1949 or business@simonandschuster.com. The Simon & Schuster Speakers Bureau can bring authors to your live event. For more information or to book an event contact the Simon & Schuster Speakers Bureau at 1-866-248-3049 or visit our website at www.simonspeakers.com. Series designed by Laura Roode. Book designed by Hannah Frece. The text of this book was set in Usherwood.
Manufactured in the United States of America 0518 FFG 10 9 8 7 6 5 4 3 2 1
Library of Congress Cataloging-in-Publication Data
Names: Green, Poppy, author. Title: Silverlake Art Show / by Poppy Green ; illustrated by Jennifer A. Bell. Description: First Little Simon paperback edition. | New York : Little Simon, 2018. | Series: The adventures of Sophie Mouse ; 13 | Summary: With the help of Hattie Frog and Owen Snake, Sophie Mouse puts together the first Silverlake Art Show but when the big night comes, she finds she is not the star of the show. Identifiers: LCCN 2017042600 | ISBN 9781534417243 (paperback) | ISBN 9781534417250 (hc) | ISBN 9781534417267 (eBook)
Subjects: | CYAC: Art—Exhibitions—Fiction. | Artists—Fiction. | Service learning—Fiction. | Mice—Fiction. | Animals—Fiction. | BISAC: JUVENILE FICTION / Animals / Mice, Hamsters, Guinea Pigs, etc. | JUVENILE FICTION / Nature & the Natural World / General (see also headings under Animals). JUVENILE FICTION / Readers / Chapter Books. Classification: LCC PZ7.G82616 Sil 2018 | DDC [Fic]—dc23 LC record available at https://lccn.loc.gov/2017042600

the adventures of
SOPHIE MOUSE

13

Silverlake Art Show

By Poppy Green • Illustrated by Jennifer A. Bell

LITTLE SIMON
New York London Toronto Sydney New Delhi

Contents

Chapter 1

Morning Masterpiece

The surface of Forget-Me-Not Lake was as smooth as glass. It reflected the colorful morning sky like a mirror.

Sophie Mouse dipped her brush into the gray-blue paint. She touched it to the canvas. It was her first brush-stroke of the day.

There was nothing to distract her. No breeze ruffled the water or the wildflowers. No other animals were about. It was still early. Soon water birds might show up to splash and play. And before long, Sophie's friends Hattie Frog and Owen Snake would arrive. The day before, they had made plans to meet for rafting and swimming. Sophie had come early to paint in the peace and quiet. She lost track

of time as she studied each part of the landscape: the different shades of yellow in the sky, the shapes of the shadows in the marsh grass, the glints of sunlight on the water.

Sophie mixed a dozen different

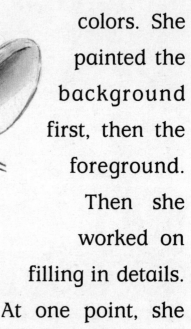

colors. She painted the background first, then the foreground. Then she worked on filling in details. At one point, she stepped back from the canvas to look at her work. "Hmm, maybe too much yellow?" Sophie asked herself aloud.

"I don't think so," someone suddenly replied.

Sophie jumped and whirled around.

It was Hattie, with Owen at her side.

"Sorry! Did I startle you?" Hattie asked.

"Didn't you hear us coming?" Owen

added. "Hattie was even humming."

Sophie shook her head and smiled. "I guess I was really concentrating."

Hattie and Owen stared at Sophie's painting. "Wow!" Owen said. "*That* is one of your best."

Hattie nodded. "Definitely," she agreed.

Sophie's whiskers twitched with satisfaction. She loved to paint. It always made her feel happy and confident. But she *especially* liked the way this painting was turning out. Sophie imagined looking at it later, at home. She thought she'd be able to feel the beautiful lake morning all over again.

Sophie washed her brushes. She packed up her paints. She left her canvas on the easel to dry.

"Ready to hit the water?" she asked her friends.

"Ready if you are!" Hattie

exclaimed.

Sophie pushed her way through wildflowers to the edge of the lake. She found her raft tied up in a little inlet. That's where she left it after each outing.

Owen and Hattie had made the raft just for her. Once upon a time,

they had tried to teach Sophie to swim. But unlike painting, swimming wasn't something she felt confident about.

Sophie was good with a paddle, though!

She stepped lightly onto her raft. Owen and Hattie jumped into the water.

"On your mark. Get set . . . ,"

Sophie called. She held her oar, ready to row. "Go!"

— Chapter 2 —

A Wise Challenge

Inside Silverlake Elementary, pencils tapped and scratched on paper. A chair creaked as someone shifted. Everyone was hard at work. It was journal-writing time.

"I'd like to read about what you did over the weekend," Mrs. Wise had told them. "And please remember include details! Lots of adjectives!"

Sophie had already written a whole paragraph about the lake. She used adjectives like *sunny, calm,* and *peaceful*—but also *splashy, fun,* and *silly*. She looked over at Hattie at the next desk. Their eyes met. Hattie winked. Sophie bet she was writing about the lake too.

It was nearing the end of the school day. Mrs. Wise asked the class to pass their journals forward. As they did, she began to write on the board. *Here comes the homework assignment,* thought Sophie.

But when Mrs. Wise stepped aside, all it said was COMMUNITY CHALLENGE.

"Class, we have an important project this week," Mrs. Wise explained. "So I will not be assigning any *written* homework."

Some students let out squeals or chirps of joy. But Mrs. Wise held up her wing to ask for quiet.

She went on. "Instead, I have a challenge for you. I would like each of you to plan and complete a community service project. Think of some way to help Silverlake Forest. You could help a neighbor with a

chore. You could help solve a prob-
lem. You all have lots of talent. Come
up with a way to give back to our
community."

Around the classroom, students
turned to one another. Whispers

grew into a murmur of voices. They were asking, sharing, wondering: What kind of project would they do?

Mrs. Wise chuckled. "You have until tomorrow to let me know what your project will be," she said.

Zoe fluttered off her seat and raised her wing. "I think I know!" she exclaimed. "My mom delivers groceries to old Mr. Badger. He lives at the edge of town. I could go with her to lend a wing! Would that work?"

What a perfect use of Zoe's flight! thought Sophie. Mrs. Wise nodded approvingly.

In the front row, Sophie's brother, Winston, raised his hand next. "I

could clean up at the playground,"
he said. "Some branches fell during
the last storm."

Sophie smiled. Winston spent lots
of time at that playground near their
house. It would be a great project for
him.

"And I'll help!" called out James Rabbit, one of Winston's best friends. "The monkey bars could use a fresh coat of paint. And I just got a new paintbrush."

Sophie didn't know James painted. What a fun idea!

Then Hattie spoke up. "I could plant some flowers by the post office." Hattie loved gardening.

Willy wanted to volunteer at the library. Ellie decided to plant trees in the apple orchard. Malcolm thought he could help his new neighbors in some way.

Sophie sat back in her chair and listened. Everyone had such great ideas. How did they think of them so fast?

What should I do? she wondered. *How can I give back to Silverlake Forest?*

Chapter 3

A Creative Idea

After school, Sophie and Winston walked the long way home. It would take them past the library. Winston wanted to stop in to look for a book.

"Piper told me about it," he said to Sophie. "It's about a mouse who likes to build things. Doesn't that sound just like me?"

"It really does!" Sophie replied.

Winston was an expert fort builder.

Inside the library, Winston hurried off to the young readers' section. Sophie headed for the check-out desk.

I ♥ Books

"Hi, Mrs. Reeve," Sophie said to the librarian. "Does the library have books on community service?" She told Mrs. Reeve about their challenge from Mrs. Wise.

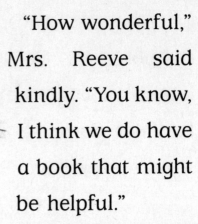

"How wonderful," Mrs. Reeve said kindly. "You know, I think we do have a book that might be helpful."

She motioned for Sophie to follow her. Then Mrs. Reeve led the way to the young readers' section. She stopped in front of the nonfiction shelves. "Now let me see . . . oh yes! Here it is!" Mrs. Reeve pulled out a book and handed it to Sophie.

Sophie read the title out loud. *"Helping Hands: Ten Ways to Give Back to Your Community."* She looked up at Mrs. Reeve and smiled. "Sounds perfect! Thank you!"

"You're very welcome," Mrs. Reeve replied. Then she headed back to the check-out desk.

Sophie sat down in a comfy reading chair. She opened the book and scanned the table of contents.

Chapter 1: Neighbors Helping Neighbors. Sophie thought that sounded like what Zoe and Malcolm were planning.

Chapter 2: Sprucing Up Public Spaces. "Like what Hattie, James, and Winston are going to do," Sophie said.

Then Sophie read the title

of chapter three: *Organizing a Community Event.*

Sophie looked up from the book. A community event? Like a party? Or a picnic? Or a show? That sounded like fun. And different. No one had mentioned anything like that in class.

"But what kind of event?" Sophie asked herself.

What was it Mrs. Wise had said? Something about using their talents.

"My talents," Sophie said, thinking it over. "Like . . . painting? An art event?" Then she sat up straight in her chair. "Wait! That's it!"

Just then Winston peeked around a bookshelf. "I found what I was looking for," he said.

Sophie closed her book and stood up. "Me too!" she replied. "Winston, I'm going to put on an art show."

Winston looked surprised. "Oh, wow! Like a show of all of your paintings?"

"Not just mine!" Sophie replied excitedly. "Everyone's! The Silverlake Art Show!"

Chapter 4

Calling All Artists

The next morning, Sophie smiled as she drizzled honey on her oatmeal. *An art show,* she thought dreamily.

From her chair at the table, Sophie stared out the window. She could see it now.

Paintings and drawings hung on a white wall. Music played softly—a violin or a cello. Platters of elegant food were passed around: tea and lemonade, tarts and tiny sandwiches.

And there, front and center, was Sophie's painting. In her mind's eye, it was her finest work—a brand-new, extra-special painting.

What would it be like to see it in

an art show, next to other artists'
work?

But wait. Sophie
snapped out of
her daydream.
She frowned.
Would anyone
else sign up?

She looked
across the table at
Winston. "*You'll* sign
up to be in the art show,
won't you?"

Winston put down his oatmeal
spoon. "Of course!" he replied—like

he couldn't believe she had to ask.

Sophie smiled. "Thanks, Winston. That's two of us, at least."

Sophie quickly made a sign-up sheet to bring to school.

Sophie wrote her name on the first line. Winston wrote his on the second. She hoped at least a few classmates would add theirs.

At school, Mrs. Wise passed out morning math worksheets. "Please work on these quietly," she told them.

"Meanwhile, I'll call each of you up to tell me your project idea."

Soon it was Sophie's turn. She brought the sign-up sheet to show Mrs. Wise.

"It will be a community art show," Sophie explained. "Anyone can

submit art to dis-
play. And anyone
can come to see
it!" Sophie paused.
"I just hope others
will sign up."

Mrs. Wise smiled
at Sophie. "I think it is
an excellent idea," she said.

The teacher cleared her throat
and addressed the whole class.

"Students, I am putting some
information on Sophie's project here."
Mrs. Wise put the sign-up sheet on a
side table, along with a pencil. "When

your worksheet is complete, you may come up and read it. Quietly, please."

Sophie returned to her desk. She felt curious eyes on her as she focused on her math.

When Sophie was done, she put her pencil down. She looked up.

Hattie's sister, Lydie, and James Rabbit were at the side table. They were looking at the sign-up sheet.

Sophie saw Lydie pick up the pencil. She was signing up!

Then James did too!

Sophie did a little happy dance in her seat. Next to her, Hattie looked

at her curiously. Then Hattie got up and went to the side table.

Sophie watched as Hattie read the sign-up sheet.

Then she picked up the pencil. She was signing up too!

Hattie returned to her seat and gave Sophie two thumbs up.

Sophie was so excited. That was three more artists! Plus Winston and herself made five. She couldn't wait until recess. She hoped she could get Owen to sign up too.

Out of the corner of her eye, Sophie saw someone else heading for the side table.

It was Mrs. Wise. She was holding up her red marking pencil. She was writing her name on the sheet!

Sophie's mouth fell open. Mrs. Wise wanted to be in her art show!

— Chapter 5 —

Sophie the Event Planner

"This is actually going to happen!" Sophie cried.

She was walking down the school-house steps with Hattie and Owen. Winston was right behind them.

Owen was holding the sign-up sheet. Hattie pointed at it. "Six artists already!" she said.

"Seven!" Owen said. He handed

the sheet to Sophie. Owen had added his name under Mrs. Wise's.

Sophie clapped for joy. "Now I'd better figure out where to have it," Sophie said. "But I have an idea." She started to run off—then stopped and turned around. "Want to come see?" she asked them. "There'll be snacks."

Hattie, Owen, and Winston nodded. So Sophie led the way. She took

the path toward the center of town.
Then she blazed a shortcut through
the Buttercup Patch. The friends
came out right near the back door
of Lily Mouse's bakery.

The aroma of fresh bread wafted through the open windows.

"Hi, Mom!" Sophie called as they entered the kitchen.

Lily Mouse was peeking into an oven. She looked up and beamed at the sight of visitors.

"Hello!" Mrs. Mouse called merrily. "Have a seat. I'll bring over the whoops tray."

The whoops tray was where Lily Mouse put the treats that hadn't turned out quite right. Some were the wrong shape or broken or lopsided.

But they were perfectly delicious.

Sophie chose a flower cookie with one petal missing. Winston and  Owen reached for broken cheesecake tarts. And Hattie picked an éclair with no filling.

Then as Hattie, Owen, and Winston nibbled, Sophie turned to her mother.

"Mom," said Sophie, "could I have an art show here at the

bakery? On Friday? With fancy food? And lemonade? And maybe music?"

"Whoa, whoa, whoa!" Lily Mouse said with a laugh. "Slow down, please. And say all that again."

Sophie was too excited to say it slowly. But she explained all about the Community Challenge. "This is my idea for a project. An art show for everyone!"

Sophie's mom loved the idea. "I would be honored to host your event," she replied.

Mrs. Mouse offered to dress up the café tables with fancy tablecloths.

She said she could bake up some special treats. "You could leave the sign-up sheet here," Mrs. Mouse suggested. "Maybe some customers will be interested."

Sophie threw her arms around her mom. "Thank you, thank you, thank you!"

The art show was coming together. She had a place. She had a date. She had artists.

Now she needed to spread the word.

Chapter 6

Helping Hands

Over the next few days, Pine Needle Grove bustled with activity.

On Tuesday afternoon, Sophie went all over town putting up posters for the art show.

And everywhere Sophie went, she saw classmates busy with the Community Challenge. She saw Willy pulling a wagon full of books.

"I'm doing a book drive for the library," Willy told Sophie. "I'm starting with all the books I don't need anymore."

Sophie met Zoe coming out of the general store with her mom. They each had a full grocery bag.

"We're taking these to Mr. Badger's house," Zoe told her. "And we'll see if any of his neighbors need anything."

Then in the distance, she spied Winston, James, and Ben heading toward the playground. Winston had some empty sacks thrown over his shoulder. The two bunny brothers were lugging paint cans. Sophie wondered what colors they had picked for the monkey bars.

After school on Wednesday, Sophie and Owen helped Hattie with her project. Hattie had dug up plants and flowers from her own garden. She was going to put them in the wooden planters around town.

They started by weeding the planter in front of the post office.

Piper zipped over carrying a bag of envelopes. She stopped to say hello. "I'm doing my mail carrier's route this week," Piper said. "Do you know she hasn't taken a day off in years?"

Piper told Hattie she'd just seen her sister, Lydie.

"She was helping Malcolm with his project," Piper said. "They're digging a root cellar for the new hedgehog family."

Later, Sophie skipped into the bakery to check the sign-up sheet. There were three more names: Ellie, Zoe, and Mrs. Follet, the bookstore owner!

On Thursday after school, Sophie and Hattie helped Owen with his project. He had a plan for making a walking path through the Buttercup Patch.

First, they collected lots of wide, flat stones. These would be the step-ping stones.

Then they mapped out a good route for the path to take around the Buttercup Patch. And then they started clearing the route.

They moved sticks and pulled up grass and weeds. Some buttercups had to be dug up too. Hattie replanted a few, off the path. Sophie offered to take the rest home.

"Just think of all the buttercup yellow paint I can make," she told them.

The work was hard and the day was warm. But by dinnertime, all the stepping stones were in place. The path was complete.

"Wow!" said Owen. "I didn't think we'd get this much done. Someday, maybe I'll make it longer."

But already it made for a lovely place to take a stroll. Everyone in town could come and enjoy it.

On the way home, Sophie stopped at the bakery again. She checked the sign-up sheet.

Sophie could not believe her eyes. All the lines were filled!

There were many new names since the day before. Willy! Willy's mom too! Mr. Handy from Handy's

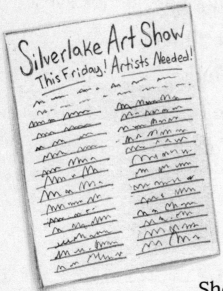

Hardware. Mrs. Weaver, the seamstress. Even Mrs. Reeve, the librarian!

Sophie's mind was racing.

Should she put out a new sign-up sheet? How many more artists would sign up the next day?

Then she gasped.

Tomorrow was Friday. Friday was the day of the show!

Double gasp!

What about her own piece of art for the show? She hadn't had a chance to work on it. And time was running out!

Chapter 7

A Long Evening

Back at home, the Mouse family sat down to a quick cold supper: radish sandwiches and a salad of fiddle-head ferns. Then Sophie planned to return to the bakery with Mrs. Mouse. They needed to do some setup that evening. On Friday, Sophie would be in school until three o'clock. That left only an hour before the art show began at four.

"James is so excited about tomorrow, Sophie," Winston
said, his mouth full
of ferns. "He has
been working on
his painting *all*
week. He's really
proud of it."

"When will I
find time to work on my painting?"
Sophie wondered out loud.

Lily Mouse smoothed the fur on
Sophie's head. "Why don't you stay
home and paint?" she suggested.

"Your dad and Winston and I can handle the setup."

Mr. Mouse and Winston nodded in agreement.

"Aw, thanks," Sophie said. "But that doesn't seem right. It is my project. I should go too."

Mr. Mouse stood up from the table. "Then how about we all go together. Four mice could make quick work of it, right?"

Sophie grinned. Maybe she *could* get home early enough to paint, after all. "Okay," Sophie said. "Let's go!"

Full of energy, the family walked together down the path to the town. Mr. Mouse whistled a tune, and they all stepped in time.

Their first task was to set up the

food tables. Sophie decided where she wanted them. Mr. and Mrs. Mouse moved them into place. Then Sophie changed her mind. So they rearranged them. Sophie shrugged.

"Maybe they were fine where they were to begin with," she said. "Sorry."

Mrs. Mouse gave Winston the tablecloths. He started spreading them on tables. Mrs. Mouse moved to the kitchen to work on the food. And Mr. Mouse started hanging wall hooks for the art. Sophie bounced between them.

"Winston," Sophie said, "I think these table-cloths are upside down."

"Oops," said Winston. "I'll fix them!"

Sophie then helped her mom whip up batter for six dozen red currant cookies. They sliced tomatoes and bread for sandwiches. It took a long time to slice the tomatoes extra thin. It took even more time to cut the crusts off all the bread. But in the end, the sandwiches looked very fancy.

Sophie went back out to help her dad. There was no hammer in the bakery toolbox, so he was using the heel of his shoe to tap the hooks in. Sophie and Winston laughed at the sight.

"Dad, could you put a hook right

here?" Sophie asked.
She pointed to an
especially well-lit
spot. Secretly, she
thought it would
be perfect for
her masterpiece.
People would be
sure to notice it
there.

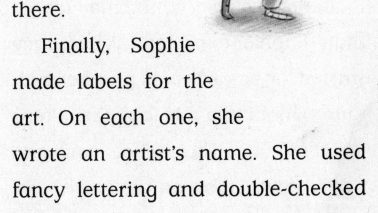

Finally, Sophie
made labels for the
art. On each one, she
wrote an artist's name. She used
fancy lettering and double-checked

her spelling. She left space so artists could write in the title of their piece.

In the end, everything took longer than Sophie expected. When they started for home, it was past her bedtime. The family retraced their steps up the path. Their pace was certainly slower than on the way there!

Mr. Mouse didn't have the energy to whistle.

And when they got home, Sophie didn't have the energy to paint.

— Chapter 8 —

The Big Day

The next morning, Sophie cut a piece from a roll of brown paper. She laid the paper on her bed. Then Sophie took down the painting of Forget-Me-Not Lake that she'd done on Sunday. She wrapped it for the art show.

Sophie sighed. She'd had her heart set on painting something special for the show. But she *did* love this painting. She knew she should feel proud to show it off.

Winston had decided on his art too. It was a sketch he'd once drawn for a four-story tree house. Slides, ladders, and spiral stairs connected the levels. The tree house hadn't been built—yet. Winston still dreamed that someday it would be.

"Good choice!" Sophie exclaimed. It was the perfect piece to represent Winston's love of building.

They both gave their pieces to Lily Mouse. She tucked them under her arm, but before she headed off to work, Sophie stopped her. She wanted to make extra certain that her mom understood where to hang hers.

Sophie and Winston went the other

way, toward Silverlake Elementary.

The classroom was abuzz with excitement. James ran up to Sophie. He said he couldn't wait for four o'clock! Hattie and Owen told Sophie they'd come early to help. It seemed like almost everyone was coming— and bringing their family.

Only Ellie seemed unsure. "I have a flute lesson after school today," she said. She looked so upset. "When it's done, I'm going to race over to the art show. But I'm not sure I'll get there in time."

Sophie knew Ellie was an excellent

flute player. She had been to one of Ellie's flute recitals.

Suddenly, Sophie had an idea.

"Ellie," Sophie said, "this might sound strange. But could you have your lesson at the art show?"

Ellie looked very confused.

Sophie explained: "Then we could

have music at the show. And we'd have *you* there!"

"Aha!" Ellie said, smiling. "I'll ask my teacher!"

Everything was ready at the bakery. Sophie, Winston, Hattie, and Owen had arrived extra early. They'd hung their own art pieces on the wall.

Hattie's was a small quilt that she had made a year ago with her mom's help.

Owen's was an abstract splatter painting.

Lily Mouse had put out the red currant cookies and tomato sandwiches. Sophie had mixed up some raspberry lemonade in a large punch bowl.

A few minutes before four, the bell on the bakery door jingled. In came Lydie, followed by Willy and his mom. Soon after, Mr. Handy and Mrs. Weaver arrived.

"Welcome, artists!" Sophie greeted them.

More artists trickled in by ones and twos. Sophie passed out the art labels. The artists added their titles. Then they each found an open hook and hung their art and labels on the wall.

Mrs. Follet's piece was a photograph of Butterfly Brook.

Mrs. Wise brought a pen-and-ink drawing of her treetop home. Many pieces were paintings. But they were all so different. There were watercolor paintings and oil paintings. There were land-scapes and portraits.

Mr. Handy's piece was a model boat made of balsa wood. Willy's was a pinch pot, a small clay bowl made by hand. Sophie set up a small table for those items, since they couldn't be hung.

Sophie marveled at the variety of the art. Silverlake Forest was a very creative community!

"Let the art show begin!" Sophie declared.

Chapter 9

Art Takes
Many Forms

Sophie Mouse looked around the bakery. She sighed with happiness—and relief. Everything was turning out just as she'd hoped.

A steady stream of animals was arriving for the art show. They moved slowly along the wall of art. They stopped to admire each piece.

The artists were all smiles as

they received many compliments.

Everyone seemed to be enjoying the delicious food.

And in one cor-ner, Ellie and her flute teacher played a duet. It was the perfect background music.

It's musical art! thought Sophie.

Then Sophie noticed a group of animals looking at something on the art wall. She watched as the crowd slowly grew bigger and bigger.

The bigger it got, the more curious Sophie became.

They're standing near my *piece,* she noticed. Sophie blushed a little bit. *Is it really that good?* She was flattered to think they were so impressed by her talent.

Sophie worked her way across the room. She squeezed her way to the front of the crowd. Yes! There was her painting of Forget-Me-Not Lake.

But it wasn't the one everyone was looking at.

They were all focused on the painting right next to it. It was a

portrait of a rabbit—a very familiar-
looking rabbit. The label read:

ARTIST: JAMES RABBIT

TITLE: MY BROTHER, BEN

"It looks just like him. Doesn't it?"
someone was saying.

"A perfect likeness," someone else said. "Wow."

Sophie had to admit, it did look like Ben. A lot. And portraits were tricky. James was obviously a very talented artist.

Sophie felt a feeling welling up inside her—a feeling she didn't want to have. She wished that a crowd was gathering in front of *her* painting. She wished they were talking about *her* talent.

Sophie was jealous.

She had said all along that this art show was for everyone. For all

of Silverlake Forest. But deep down, Sophie had secretly hoped her piece would stand out.

This is not a competition, she scolded herself. *So why do I feel like I lost?*

Just then Sophie spotted Mrs. Wise heading her way. She took a deep breath and forced a smile.

"I wanted to thank you, Sophie," said Mrs. Wise. "I've had such a wonderful time at your art show. And congratulations! You have *two* works of art on display."

Sophie looked at her quizzically. "Two?" she said. "What do you mean?"

"Well, your painting is gorgeous." said Mrs. Wise. "Really, it's spectacular!"

Sophie smiled— a real smile now. Mrs. Wise went on.

"But look around. Look how much of the community is here, together: young, old, beginners, experts, artists, and the people who love them. It's beautiful. I think this event is a real work of art."

Her words warmed Sophie's heart.
She looked around the bakery again.
And she saw that it was true.

Chapter 10

Art Class

It was another calm and peaceful Sunday morning at Forget-Me-Not Lake. The morning sky was different this time—more pink and orange. But once again, the water reflected it like a mirror.

Sophie studied the trees across the lake. She noted the shades of color in the sky, the water, and the marsh grass. She could see more than a dozen different colors. But she didn't mix her paints just yet.

Before long, she heard footsteps behind her. Sophie turned.

"Good morning, James!" she called.

"Hi!" James replied. He was lugging an easel and a blank canvas. Right behind him was Winston carrying James's art case.

"It's nice of you to help us out, Winston," Sophie said.

Winston beamed and put the case down. "Where should I sit?" he asked.

James surveyed the area. He pointed to a sunlit rock by the water.

"How about right there?" James said. Then he set up his easel and canvas next to Sophie's. He pulled out a paintbrush and a palette. "Ready?" he asked Sophie.

Sophie nodded. "Thanks for offering to show me how to paint portraits," she said.

"Thanks for showing me this great spot!" James said. "It looks just like your amazing painting. I still don't get how you mix such bright colors. But I'm excited to learn."

Sophie had a feeling they would both learn a lot today.

Then the two artists turned to their subject.

"So how long do I have to sit here?" Winston asked from his perch.

"Um . . ." Sophie looked at James.

"Not long," James said. "A couple of hours?"

"Hours?" Winston cried.

"Don't worry," Sophie said. "We'll definitely take a break for lunch. Hold still now!"

The End

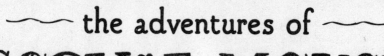

the adventures of
SOPHIE MOUSE

For excerpts, activities, and more about
these adorable tales & tails, visit
AdventuresofSophieMouse.com!

If you like Sophie Mouse, you'll love

the CRITTER club